THE BABY BLUES

Also by Janice Lee Smith

The Monster in the Third Dresser Drawer
And Other Stories About Adam Joshua

The Kid Next Door and Other Headaches
More Stories About Adam Joshua

The Show-and-Tell War
And Other Stories About Adam Joshua

It's Not Easy Being George
Stories About Adam Joshua (And His Dog)

The Turkeys' Side of It
Adam Joshua's Thanksgiving

There's a Ghost in the Coatroom
Adam Joshua's Christmas

Nelson in Love
An Adam Joshua Valentine's Day Story

Serious Science
An Adam Joshua Story

THE BABY BLUES

AN ADAM JOSHUA STORY

by Janice Lee Smith

drawings by Dick Gackenbach

HarperCollins*Publishers*

My thanks to Kathy Spurling and her great students at Kingsbury Elementary School in La Porte, Indiana. Their delightful letters about "Adopt an Egg Week" were hilarious, inspiring, and an enormous help in writing this book.

The Baby Blues
Text copyright © 1994 by Janice Lee Smith
Illustrations copyright © 1994 by Dick Gackenbach

Library of Congress Cataloging-in-Publication Data
Smith, Janice Lee, date
    The baby blues : an Adam Joshua story / by Janice Lee Smith ; drawings by Dick Gackenbach.
        p.   cm.
    Summary: Adam Joshua and his classmates' anxiety over the approaching maternity leave of their favorite teacher Ms. D. is heightened when they are each assigned an egg baby in a class project about parenting.
    ISBN 0-06-023642-6. — ISBN 0-06-023643-4 (lib. bdg.)
    [1. Babies—Fiction.   2. Eggs—Fiction.   3. Schools—Fiction.]   I. Gackenbach, Dick, ill.   II. Title.
PZ7.S6499Bab   1994   93-14492
[Fic]—dc20   CIP
                                                                AC

Typography by Al Cetta
1   2   3   4   5   6   7   8   9   10
❖
First Edition

To all the great great-grand Lees
Chandra and Scott
Kristen
P.S. That is Great-Grandma Olivia on
page 68.
P.P.S. Great-Grandpa Jim is too much of a
character to fit into this book!

Chapter One

Adam Joshua and his dog, George, agreed most of the time about most things, but there was one thing they agreed about absolutely the most.

"Nobody should have to live in the same house with a two-year-old," Adam Joshua said. "And nobody should even have to live in the same country with Amanda Jane."

George felt exactly the same, and fairly

weary besides. It was only Monday morning, but it was already turning into a long week.

Just yesterday, which should have been his day off, he'd been wrestled into a dress, locked in a closet, and nearly flushed by Amanda Jane.

"And it's bad enough that it's bad enough with a baby at home," Adam Joshua said, "but what's happening at school is even worse. Ms. D.'s getting ready to have *her* baby now and that means she's going to leave. Everybody's very upset."

George was sorry to hear it, but he had his own problems. Amanda Jane had also poured honey all over him and then cornflakes and tiny marshmallows all over that. Then George had to have a bath, and even though he was never so glad to have a bath in his life, it was still a bath and he hated baths. Especially this one since Amanda Jane got to help.

"I'm the most upset," Adam Joshua told George. "Ms. D.'s the best teacher I've ever had, and I'm doing the best in school I've ever done. Now everything's going to change."

He shook his head sadly. He still couldn't believe that Ms. D. was going to abandon him for some baby she hadn't even met yet.

"Ms. D. also keeps people like Elliot Banks from causing as much trouble as they want to, and she loves my jokes and hearing all about you," Adam Joshua told George.

George certainly hoped somebody had told her about what was happening to him lately. After the bath he'd tried hiding out in the laundry room. But he hadn't been paying enough attention because he had a bad headache and was still trying to get junk out of his fur, and Amanda Jane had come along and stuffed him into the dryer

before he knew what hit him.

"The substitute will probably think Elliot's great, hate jokes and dogs, and hate
me even more," Adam Joshua said, very
glum.

A load of wet towels had landed on top
of George and it was only luck and a lot of
howling that had stopped Adam Joshua's
mother from putting him through fluff and
dry.

All things considered, he wasn't the
same dog he'd been last week.

"I'm sorry," Adam Joshua said, giving
George a hug. "If it's any help, Mom says
Amanda Jane won't be two forever."

Nobody could have any idea how relieved George was to know that.

"Of course three might be even worse,"
Adam Joshua told him.

Adam Joshua's best friend, Nelson, had a
two-year-old at his house too.

"I don't think I should even have to be on the same planet with Henry," Nelson said as they walked to school. "I don't know why anybody ever has a baby to begin with."

Adam Joshua certainly couldn't understand why his parents had had Amanda Jane. They already had him.

For that matter, he couldn't understand why Ms. D. wanted a baby either. She already had him too.

"My mom said we could have the baby shower on Friday," Heidi was saying as Adam Joshua and Nelson walked into the classroom. "Since Mr. D. always brings Ms. D. to school, we'll have it right after they get here so they both can be surprised."

Most people nodded, excited. It'd be a terrific party with Mr. D. around.

Personally, Adam Joshua planned to be somewhere else because he didn't feel the least bit like having a party for this baby. On the other hand, the party was at school and he was supposed to be at school, so he hadn't figured out yet where the somewhere else was going to be.

"My mom says that she'll bring a cake, because a little cake after breakfast won't hurt this once," Heidi told them. "Then the other room mother will bring punch, and we're all supposed to get here early and hide our gifts so everything will be a surprise."

Adam Joshua decided he might stay at the party long enough to have a little cake.

"My mom says that even though it's a few weeks before Ms. D. leaves to have the baby, you never can tell about babies, so that's why we should have the party this week," Heidi said.

Everybody looked gloomy about Ms. D. leaving anytime.

Then Elliot Banks walked in the door

and they all switched to looking disgusted instead.

Elliot always smirked, but he'd advanced to a supersmirk since Ms. D. was getting ready to leave.

"Nearly time for Ms. D. to be gone," he said, adding a sneer while he was about it. "With Ms. D. gone things are going to go my way."

Adam Joshua had seen Elliot's way before. It wasn't a direction he cared for.

"You," Elliot said, poking a finger in Adam Joshua's chest. "I've got a lot to teach you."

A.J. had a pretty good idea of the stuff Elliot wanted to teach him. It wasn't stuff he had any desire to know at all.

They heard Ms. D.'s voice in the hall, so everybody scurried to their desks and tried to look angelic and ready to learn lots of things.

Ms. D. used to bustle when she came in the doorway, but lately it had slowed down to more of a waddle.

"I've never known anybody that pregnant," Angie whispered.

"Me too, either," Mr. D. said from somewhere behind Ms. D.

"Me too, too," Ms. D. said, sighing as she tried three times to get settled behind her desk.

Mr. D. put down all the books and bags he'd carried in for Ms. D. and looked like he was thinking of settling in along with her.

He'd turned into a terrible worrier. Besides bringing Ms. D. to school in the mornings, he picked her up in the afternoons, and some days he dropped by for lunch, and some days he just dropped by to drop by.

"In fact, you're getting to be a real pest," Angie told him.

"Hey!" Mr. D. yelped. "I know it's not for a few weeks yet, but I want to be around in case Ms. D. decides to have the baby."

"If she has one we'll call you," Angie told him sternly, pointing toward the door.

Everybody was so nervous about the thought of Ms. D. having the baby while they weren't looking, they were finding it hard to get their worksheets or much of anything else done.

A lot of people kept going up to her desk to ask her questions, and a lot of people went up to give her advice, and the rest just kept a good close eye on her.

Personally, Adam Joshua was keeping both eyes on her.

Evidently Ms. D. had finally decided that enough was enough.

"You all need a project to keep you busy," she told them at the end of the day.

"Or rather I need for you to have a project to keep you busy."

Everybody looked a little confused, but they were ready enough to hear about the project.

"So," Ms. D. said, placing one of her bags on the corner of her desk, "you're going to get a chance to be parents yourselves."

Everybody looked at the bag in total panic. Nobody felt that they were doing that great as a brother or sister. Being a parent sounded like more than they could handle.

"Excuse me," Angie said anxiously, "but if there's a baby in there, I don't want one."

Nobody wanted one, and it got noisy for a minute while everybody said so.

"Close." Ms. D. laughed as she took cartons out of the bag.

"Egg-babies," she said, taking eggs out of the cartons.

Nobody seemed to know if they felt relieved.

"You're going to be in charge of your egg just like a parent is in charge of a real baby," Ms. D. told them. "And your assignment is to keep it with you all the time, and keep it safe from harm, and let it know you love it."

"I've never known any eggs except scrambled," Angie said doubtfully. "I'm not sure I want to be a mother to one."

A lot of people nodded, and a lot of others shook their heads, but they all meant that they agreed with Angie.

"You'll want to give it a face and a personality and a name," Ms. D. told them anyway.

The egg she handed Adam Joshua looked to him like the runt of the litter. He couldn't believe Ms. D. was asking him to be its father. He had enough trouble being a person to his dog, George, and a brother to Amanda Jane.

"But how hard can it be?" Sidney asked, taking his egg with a shrug.

"You need a project too," Ms. D. told Mr. D., giving him an egg when he came by to pick her up. "It'll be good practice for the baby."

"No problem," Mr. D. said smugly. "I've been reading books. I've been studying up. I've even taken some father classes."

He stuck the egg in his shirt pocket.

"Perfectly safe," he said, giving it a little pat. "Anybody need any advice on how to take care of their egg, just ask the expert dad."

Several people scurried over to ask.

Mr. D. gave Ms. D. a big hug and then he got a funny look on his face.

Egg yolk dribbled out of his pocket and ran down his shirt front.

All the people who'd scurried over looked horrified and hurried away again.

"Fatherhood may not be all it's cracked up to be," Mr. D. said glumly, as Ms. D. handed him some paper towels.

It took Adam Joshua and Nelson twice as long as it usually did to walk home because they went carefully with their eggs, stepping around every crack and bump on the way.

"I don't think this is going to work out," Nelson said. "I've got enough problems at home with a real baby. The last thing I need is this egg."

Since the dryer disaster George had decided to spend more time across the street visiting his favorite dog, Lucy. But he kept watch and as soon as he saw Adam Joshua coming home after school, George went charging down the sidewalk to say hello.

There were a few interesting moments while Adam Joshua tried to keep the egg out of George's way.

"I have to take care of this and keep it safe," Adam Joshua explained, finally sitting on George to keep him quiet.

George looked a little miffed. Besides being sat on, he wasn't used to an egg getting in the way of his afternoon attention.

"Ms. D. asked me to," Adam Joshua told George. "Everybody has to take care of one. It's like homework."

George looked better. He liked Ms. D. a lot and usually anything she said was good enough for him.

"And I'll need your help when I'm home," Adam Joshua said. "Ms. D. didn't mention it, but I know she was counting on you."

George looked satisfied. He should have expected he'd be counted on, and he wasn't the kind of dog to let Ms. D. down.

"Especially around Amanda Jane," Adam Joshua said, getting up off of George.

When he opened their front door, they both stuck their heads in cautiously. Amanda Jane didn't seem to be around, but that didn't mean she wasn't around. Even for a two-year-old she was sneaky.

Adam Joshua and George started creeping up the stairs.

"Swaddledorp," said a sweet little voice behind them.

They made it up to the bedroom with Amanda Jane hot on their trail.

"Zappadorpdiffle!" she hollered, banging on the other side of the door the minute Adam Joshua slammed it shut.

Adam Joshua and George sat for a while and stared at their egg.

Adam Joshua had no idea what the father of poultry was supposed to do. It didn't seem to him that the egg had much personality at all, and he could tell George didn't think so, either.

Still, since it didn't have a face yet, it might not be fair to judge.

He did his best, but the egg was so small, he ended up drawing little eyes close together and a tiny mouth. By the time he was finished, it had a personality that was downright scary, and it looked a tad bald.

"So hair might help," Adam Joshua said, cutting a little hair off George's tail before George even saw it coming.

George was absolutely outraged. Things were hard enough lately, and as much as he liked Ms. D., he thought she was carrying this counting-on-him thing a little too far.

Chapter Two

Adam Joshua woke up the next morning with an egg staring him in the face.

And it looked mad, mean, and like it could get to be a real hard-boiled character.

George woke up, took one look at it, and growled back.

Adam Joshua named it Waldo.

"I've always hated that name," he told George.

Nelson showed up for their school walk with the ugliest egg Adam Joshua had ever seen. He just hoped he never had to meet one like it at breakfast.

"I got a little carried away," Nelson said, looking at his egg's sharp, pointed teeth and crooked nose. "But I didn't want Sneed to turn out cute."

Adam Joshua didn't think Nelson had a thing to worry about.

"I mean, I've been thinking about it a lot and I'm pretty sure this whole baby thing has to do with cute," Nelson said. "Everybody thinks babies are cute, so everybody wants one. It's like a disguise. You can't tell they're dangerous at all. Then they get dangerous just a little bit at a time, but they still stay cute so they can get away with anything."

Adam Joshua knew it was true. Amanda Jane got away with an awful lot of stuff because she was cute. On the other hand, he didn't think he had a bit of cute left in him and he hardly ever got away with a thing.

"My baby brother, Henry, is as cute as they come," Nelson said, sighing.

A lot of people were already in the classroom when Adam Joshua and Nelson got there. Everyone was moving slowly and carefully with their egg-babies.

Angie's was all snuggled down in a little basket with a tiny teddy bear tucked in beside it.

"I've named her Scarlett," Angie said, showing it to Adam Joshua. "And she stayed alive a whole night, which is more than some of my hamsters ever did."

Heidi had a great Chinese-looking egg.

"This is Egg Fu Yung," she said, introducing her around.

Jonesy's egg had evil eyes and fangs, and it was wearing a black cape.

"Dracuegg," Jonesy said, cackling. "He's

going to suck the yolk right out of your kids."

Nate's egg had crossed eyes, an enormous nose, and green and purple yarn hair. "His name is Zilch," Nate said proudly. "He's going to grow up to be the drummer in a rock band."

"Don't even ask," Sidney said, pouring a lot of yolk out of his backpack.

When they got to the classroom, Mr. D. backed up to let Ms. D. try the doorway alone.

"No offense, but we've gotten stuck a few times lately," Mr. D. said, chuckling. "It's probably my fault. I've been putting on a bit of weight lately."

"Right," Ms. D. grumbled.

Mr. D.'s second egg looked just like Mr. D.

"Except shorter, rounder, and smoother," Sidney told him.

"And babies usually don't have beards," said Angie.

Mr. D.'s egg also had three bandages across the top of its head.

"Headache?" asked Sidney.

"Concussion," sighed Mr. D.

As soon as Ms. D. had done her settling in, a lot of people, including Mr. D., crowded around her to ask for new eggs.

"So many?" Ms. D. laughed. "So soon?"

"I didn't even make it home with my egg, Edwina," Gabby told Ms. D. sadly. "First a little kid ran into me on the sidewalk and I dropped my egg and all the insides fell out. I tried to carry a lot of the shell home, and I glued it all together."

Gabby sighed and a tear slid down her cheek. "Edwina came out a lot smaller and a bit square," she said, "so I shortened her name and put her up on the shelf to dry and then . . ."

Gabby gave a great gulp, burst into tears, and threw herself into Ms. D.'s arms. "I left the room for just a minute," she sobbed. "And when I came back my cat, Mystery, was eating the last of Ed."

Ms. D. dried Gabby off, then gave her a hug and another egg.

"Thank you," Gabby said. "My mother said Mystery must need more vitamins, but I'll make sure she doesn't get this egg."

Sidney stepped up after Gabby.

"My cat needed vitamins too," he told Ms. D., giving a great fake sob and wiping at his dry eyes.

"My cat," sobbed Philip.

"My cat," sobbed Doug.

"Our cat ate it," Mr. D. sobbed as he held out his hand for an egg.

"We don't have a cat," Ms. D. reminded him.

"It sounds like we definitely should get

one," Mr. D. told her as he headed out the door.

Adam Joshua tried to keep one eye on Waldo and one eye on Ms. D. while he worked, and it wasn't long before he was feeling cross-eyed.

Lunch came as a big relief, although trying to protect an egg on the lunch table and eat spaghetti at the same time was no picnic.

Everybody else talked about Ms. D.'s party.

Most of the boys were getting gifts for a baby boy.

"I'm getting him a baby blanket," Nate said proudly. "A baby needs a blanket a lot. And a blanket lasts a long time, so he'll have it when he gets older, for when he goes to school and gets married and stuff."

He pulled a ratty, tattered blanket out of his backpack to show them. "See," he

said. "I plan to give it to my own son someday."

Nobody made fun of the blanket since they all had things in their backpacks that were a lot worse.

Most of the girls were getting gifts for a baby girl.

"I'm getting her a toolbox," Heidi said firmly. "It's taken me forever to get a toolbox, and I don't want the baby to have to go through the same thing."

Several people were getting gifts for Mr. D.

"I'm getting two really great bath ducks," Gabby said. "That way there's one for Mr. D. so he and the baby won't fight."

Jonesy, Philip, and Sidney were getting together to get Mr. D. a skateboard.

"Because the baby will take all of Ms. D.'s time," said Jonesy.

"And get in Mr. D.'s toys and mess everything up," said Philip.

"And blame everything on Mr. D," said Sidney.

"So Mr. D.'s going to have to get out of the house a lot," said Jonesy.

"And he's going to feel really lonely and bored and have nothing to do," said Philip.

"And now with a skateboard he'll feel a lot better," Sidney said, very pleased.

Waldo didn't look any too happy about heading home after school. Adam Joshua wasn't any happier about taking him.

When he got near his house, he could see that George's dog friend, Lucy, was waiting out on the sidewalk with George.

Adam Joshua wasn't all that crazy about Lucy, mostly because she took up so much of George's time. Still, he hadn't seen her a lot lately, and it was probably time to get to know her better.

He was just getting close enough to say something friendly when he got a good look at Lucy, and he nearly dropped Waldo right then and there.

Lucy had gotten fat in the middle and lumpy around the edges, and all things considered, she looked as much like Ms. D. as a dog could look.

"Isn't it a great surprise, Adam Joshua?" Lucy's owner, Mrs. Sikes, called, waving from across the street. "I think we're in for puppies any day!"

And the look George gave Adam Joshua was the same proud, goofy look Mr. D. had been walking around with for ages.

"I can't believe you didn't ask me first," Adam Joshua yelled at George when they were up in their room. "And then I can't believe you didn't even tell me."

George looked astonished that Adam Joshua felt that way about it.

"I thought we had the same ideas about babies!" Adam Joshua shouted. "I thought we felt exactly the same! Sure, they'll be cute when they're little, but do you have any idea what puppies are like when they're two?"

George didn't, but then he didn't think Adam Joshua did either.

"You're gone all the time now," Adam Joshua said. "If you have puppies, you'll be gone even more. Just look how Ms. D.'s going to be gone. Besides," he told George firmly, "you don't know a thing about being a father. You hardly know a thing about being a dog."

George looked insulted.

Adam Joshua didn't feel a bit like apologizing.

It was bath night.

And as far as Adam Joshua was concerned, and absolutely no matter what Ms. D. said, he took his baths alone without any eggs watching.

"So you have to egg-sit Waldo," he told George. "It will give you some practice."

George did his best to look trustworthy and reliable.

Waldo was glaring as much as ever.

"He's not too happy about this puppy thing," Adam Joshua told George.

Normally Adam Joshua wasn't too fond of baths, but it was nice to be away from fatherhood for a while.

He soaked a good long time and tried to stop worrying about Ms. D. abandoning him for the baby and George abandoning him for the puppies.

By the end of it all he came out of the bathroom humming while he wrapped the towel tighter around his middle.

Amanda Jane burst out of his room at high speed and went by him at a gallop, the egg in one hand and George right behind.

Adam Joshua was halfway down the

stairs after them before he remembered he
was only wearing the towel.

And it wasn't until Amanda Jane had
come to a fast stop in the living room, and
George had fallen over her, and Adam
Joshua had fallen over both of them, and
the towel had fallen off and all he was
wearing was a lot of Waldo, that he looked
up and remembered that his parents had in-

vited company over to visit for the evening.

George looked really guilty, but as far as Adam Joshua was concerned, there was no way on earth it could be guilty enough.

Chapter Three

When Adam Joshua and Nelson walked into their classroom the next morning, a lot of people were walking around looking tragic and eggless.

Heidi was dressed all in black and she was wearing a big black hat with a veil.

"It's my mother's," she said glumly. "She always wears it to funerals when somebody dies. I'm going to have a funeral for my egg in the reading corner if anybody would like to come."

A lot of people who'd lost eggs went to the funeral, and a lot of friends of the eggs went too.

Heidi started by saying a few words.

"Egg Fu Yung was always a good egg," she said softly. "And I will miss her."

"I didn't know her very well," Angie joined in. "But what I knew I liked."

Several other people who had lost their eggs stepped forward to say something nice about them. Adam Joshua couldn't think of anything good to say about Waldo, so he stayed quiet.

"I didn't like my egg all that much," Sidney said when it was his turn. "But still, I'm sorry about the lawn mower."

Mr. and Ms. D. came in the door and quietly joined the funeral.

Mr. D. borrowed Heidi's hat and veil and came forward.

"I will miss my egg, Dauntless, a great deal," he said, mourning. "He was a fine egg, and I'm sorry he had to come to such a messy, tragic end."

"What happened?" Sidney asked, breaking the hush.

"It was a shattering experience," wept Mr. D.

Mr. D. left and people started heading for their desks.

"Dracuegg bit the dust," Jonesy told everybody. "So this is my new baby, Frankenegg."

Jonesy had glued little screws and bolts all over his egg, and he'd given him eyes with a glazed, crazed look and an evil smile.

Angie made Jonesy put Frankenegg clear down at the end of the windowsill, away from all the other babies.

"He'll get them anyway," Jonesy told

her in a creaky, crawly voice.

They were all too polite to mention it, but Ms. D. was looking plumper and lumpier than ever.

It would have been better if Sidney hadn't tried to cheer her up about it.

"That's a really nice dress," he told her. "It keeps people from noticing you're so fat."

Before they got down to work, Ms. D. went to the chalkboard and she got a look on her face that they all dreaded.

"Has anybody learned anything terrific yet about taking care of their egg-babies?" Ms. D. asked, getting ready to make a list.

Everybody thought hard. They hated this part of Ms. D.'s projects, but if they didn't come up with something fast, she might make them write about it or give a talk. Ms. D. was awfully tricky when it came to this stuff.

"I've learned it's best not to skateboard

with an egg," Heidi said politely.

"Or sleep with it," Gabby said sadly.

"Or have it anywhere around when you're looking for something to throw at your brother," Nate said, disgusted.

Ms. D. sighed and looked a little stern, so everybody started thinking faster and harder.

"I've learned you can't tell who you're getting," Angie finally said. "I mean, you gave me an egg that turned out to be Scarlett, but other eggs from the same box turned out to be that awful Zilch and that creepy Waldo."

"Hey!" Nate yelped, looking really insulted for Zilch.

Since Adam Joshua hadn't been crazy about Waldo, he didn't mind an insult or two. Besides, he was too busy thinking about the rest of what Angie had said. He'd never really thought about not knowing who you'd get before, but now that he had it made incredible sense. If it was true for eggs, it must be true for babies, and it certainly explained Amanda Jane. His parents had gotten really lucky when they got him. They must have only wanted another baby because they thought they'd get somebody just like him again.

He was really very flattered.

"You don't know who you're getting either," Doug told Ms. D. "It could be anybody in there. Even somebody like my baby sister, Sarah."

Everybody, especially the big brothers and sisters, nodded solemnly.

It was a lot easier than usual to wear Ms. D. down.

"Right," she muttered, heading back to her desk.

During recess they made a nursery for the babies on the playground.

"I'll egg-sit first," Angie said. She sat by

the eggs and sang them a little "Rock-a-Bye Egg."

"They're all taking naps now," Angie whispered to Sidney when he came to take over.

Sidney sat quietly and watched the babies for a few minutes.

"Humpty Dumpty sat on a wall, had a fall, and ended up splattered over all!" he sang out loudly at the top of his voice.

The eggs survived, but Sidney nearly got scrambled by Angie.

George was waiting at home for Adam Joshua, probably because he still felt guilty about Waldo, but he was doing his best not to show it.

"This is my new baby, Barney," Adam Joshua said. "Ms. D. gave him to me after I told her what happened to Waldo."

George looked fairly alarmed that Adam Joshua had thought to mention it to Ms. D.

"Ms. D.'s very disappointed in you," Adam Joshua told George. "And she just hopes you've learned something."

George looked really terrible about disappointing Ms. D. He had no idea what she'd wanted him to learn, but he was sure he probably had.

Adam Joshua went slowly and carefully while he drew a face and Barney ended up with a smile in his eyes and a wonderful grin.

George saw it coming this time, but he was too depressed to be fast enough.

"I'd think you'd be glad to help out," Adam Joshua said, sitting firmly on George while he clipped off a little more tail hair.

Ms. D. had told them to show their eggs that they loved them, but Adam Joshua had never gotten that far with Waldo.

He decided he'd better get started with Barney, so he sang the special little song his father sometimes sang to him.

Amanda Jane and George came by while he was singing it and stopped in to listen. Amanda Jane started inching closer while Adam Joshua sang until she finally ended up in his lap with her head on his chest.

"Zedda," she told him very sweetly when he was finished. She gave him a kiss on the cheek and then ran, screeching, on her way again.

"My mother says never try to figure out a two-year-old," Adam Joshua told Barney.

He read Barney a book about a space fighter who saved the day.

"I'm sorry," Adam Joshua said, "I don't know any stories where an egg's the hero." He didn't mention it, but he didn't know any where the chicken was a hero either.

They played a few games and Adam Joshua let Barney win as often as he could.

Actually, George was a lot better at

cards than Barney was.

"Of course, he doesn't cheat like you do," Adam Joshua told George.

George was happy to hear it. He was starting to feel jealous on top of everything else, and he was glad Adam Joshua realized he did some things better than that stupid egg.

Chapter Four

Ms. D. wasn't there when they got to the classroom the next morning.

The principal, Mrs. Rodriguez, stood by the desk instead.

"She had the baby, she had the baby, oh, my gosh, she had the baby!" Sidney yelled, dropping his egg and running around in circles.

Several other people started yelling and running around in circles too.

"She didn't have the baby, she didn't have the baby!" Mrs. Rodriguez called out, trying to be heard. "She just had a doctor's appointment."

"Thank goodness!" everybody said.

"It's nice to see you too," Mrs. Rodriguez told them, laughing.

Everybody who still had an egg introduced it to Mrs. Rodriguez.

"I'm keeping a baby book for Scarlett," Angie said, showing her a few pages.

There was a picture of Scarlett bald, without a face. "Scarlett's first day at home," Angie had written under it.

There was a picture of Scarlett out in her baby carriage, and one in a sandbox, and several of her on Angie's lap.

"And here's her family," Angie said proudly, showing a lot of pages with a lot of eggs in hats, caps, frills, and mustaches.

"She'll be able to show this to her grandchildren when she's an old, old egg," Angie said.

"Give me a break," Sidney moaned, mopping up yolk.

Mrs. Rodriguez started handing out math worksheets.

"I beg your pardon," Heidi said. "We don't do math in this class."

"That's the third time I've heard that lately," Mrs. Rodriguez told her.

People hurried to take their eggs over to the nursery shelf.

"He's just so cute, Adam Joshua!" Angie said when she saw Barney.

Adam Joshua was surprised at how fatherly and proud he felt.

He noticed Nelson glaring at him.

"Sometimes cute isn't so bad," Adam Joshua told him firmly.

Nate looked around and looked puzzled.

"I can't figure out where my egg, Zilch Three, went," he said. "I had my eye on him, but he wandered off."

Mrs. Rodriguez sat down at Ms. D.'s desk. There was a loud, wet crunching sound and she got a terrible look on her face.

"Found him," said Nate.

Ms. D. came in while they were hard at work, and she looked happy enough to see them but was pretty quiet and awfully thoughtful.

"I wouldn't take my eyes off this bunch for a minute," Mrs. Rodriguez told her before she headed back to the principal's office. "They're cute but tricky."

Normally Ms. D. would have given them even more math worksheets and checked everything they'd done at least twice to make sure they'd done it right. But today she hardly seemed to notice what they were doing, and after a while some of the class rats stopped doing it and started writing notes and fiddling around instead.

Adam Joshua got a note from the biggest rat.

"Soon you're all mine," it said, and it was signed with a skull and crossbones, which meant Elliot no matter how you spelled it.

The rats got away with a lot for the rest of the morning, and Adam Joshua started wishing that Ms. D. would at least notice there were some people who weren't ratting around.

But Ms. D. kept wandering over to the window, and she looked like she was staring at something a million miles away. Several times Adam Joshua saw her smile a secret little smile. She remembered to give them more work, but her attention didn't seem to be on it.

The class rats didn't seem to mind at all.

At lunchtime Nelson added red dots to Sneed's face.

"Chicken pox," Nelson said, very proud.

Angie shrieked and scurried away with Scarlett so she wouldn't catch anything.

"It's too late," Nelson called after Angie. "Sneed's already breathed lots of terrible germs on her."

After lunch everybody else went outside, but Adam Joshua strolled down the hall and past his classroom to check on Ms. D.

She was sitting at her desk looking gloomy. Adam Joshua was thinking of strolling away again when she noticed him and smiled.

"My favorite joke-teller!" she said. "I could use some cheering up. I was just sitting here feeling a little discouraged."

Adam Joshua had had no idea that Ms. D. ever got discouraged. He couldn't think of a single joke. He stayed quiet, thought hard, and tried to look sympathetic.

"I've let myself start to worry," Ms. D. said, looking glum. "I mean, I'm going to be a mother very soon, and I'm pretty sure I'm going to be a good mother, but what if I'm not? I really don't know a lot about babies."

Adam Joshua could have told her a few things, but they weren't especially funny and he thought now might not be the time.

"I know," she said, smiling at him, "I'm a good teacher. But mostly that's because you kids are so great."

Adam Joshua tried to mix a little modesty in with his sympathetic look. He could have mentioned at least one kid who wasn't great, but he kept quiet.

Ms. D. gave him a bigger smile.

"Who could have a kid like you around and not want to have somebody just like you for their own?"

Adam Joshua tried to hold on to the modesty and the sympathy and not fall

over from absolute shock. He'd had no idea Ms. D. felt that way about him.

"You know, you're right," Ms. D. said, finally getting back to being Ms. D. again. "I'm going to love being a mother just like I've loved being a teacher, and everything and everybody's going to turn out fine."

She got up from her desk and started out the door.

"Thanks for cheering me up," she said, stopping to give Adam Joshua a hug on her way.

Adam Joshua loved his talks with Ms. D. He just wished he had some idea what they'd been talking about.

By the time people started coming inside again, Adam Joshua was the one sitting at his desk looking gloomy.

The one thing he had understood was that Ms. D. was having a baby because he was so great. That was even worse than figuring out that his parents had had Amanda Jane because of him. What if Ms. D. had someone like Amanda Jane too and it was all his fault?

He felt really guilty about being so terrific.

He thought maybe he'd better go to the baby shower after all.

Somehow it seemed like the least he could do.

"I don't think you're going to be all that terrific as a father," Adam Joshua told George after school. "Just look what happened when you were egg-sitting Waldo. It's very discouraging and you should worry."

George switched between looking worried and looking guilty and finally settled in the middle at miserable.

Adam Joshua didn't mind leaving him there at all.

Adam Joshua didn't have a gift for Ms. D.'s party and he needed one, and he needed it by tomorrow. He knew he could ask his parents to take him shopping, but he couldn't think of a single thing to buy that would be special enough for Ms. D. and her baby.

He thought hard for a long time. When he finally thought of a gift, it seemed so perfect he couldn't believe it had taken him so long.

George kept looking so miserable, Adam Joshua finally felt sorry for him.

"Let's just get back to you and me, and no Lucy and no puppies," Adam Joshua said, cuddling George. "I'll take care of you and the egg. I'm very good at it, and you can depend on me."

George stopped looking miserable and started watching something over Adam

Joshua's shoulder.

Adam Joshua turned around in time to see Amanda Jane getting Barney down from the shelf and heading out the door.

It seemed to him that Amanda Jane was getting faster every day.

First he looked down to make sure he had clothes on, and by the time he was out the door and down the stairs, Amanda Jane was sitting up on the living-room sofa reading one of her books, and there was no egg in sight.

"Zanporcodnoffradadiddle," she told him sternly.

George grinned at Adam Joshua as though he would have loved to say exactly the same thing himself.

Chapter Five

Adam Joshua woke up the next morning with Amanda Jane sitting on his stomach. Her nose was pressed against his nose and she was staring into his eyes.

It nearly scared him out of a day's growth before he'd even gotten into the day.

"Zedda," Amanda Jane said firmly.

Adam Joshua wasn't feeling full of brotherly love at the moment, but she'd sit on him all day if he didn't give her what she wanted.

He sang her his song, which was beginning to seem more like her song by the minute. Amanda Jane curled up with her head on his chest and hummed along. When he was finished, she bounced on his stomach twice and then ran on her way again.

George scooted over in the bed and put his head on Adam Joshua's chest now that it was vacant. He was getting very fond of that song, and as far as he was concerned it was about time somebody got around to singing it to him.

Adam Joshua was heading out his front door for school when Amanda Jane showed up carefully pulling her wagon. Barney was piled in the wagon with a pile of other stuff.

"Snordorf," Amanda Jane said solemnly, handing the egg to Adam Joshua.

"More snordorf," she said, handing him a lot of other things too.

"You don't even want to know," Adam Joshua told Nelson as he walked down the sidewalk carrying Barney, a stuffed pig, an egg beater, a small sneaker, and a feather duster.

The classroom was already looking like a party by the time Adam Joshua and Nelson walked in.

"Hurry and help!" Angie scolded, giving them banners, balloons, and a stern look.

Nobody argued with Angie. They got busy and started decorating like crazy.

Doug had forgotten to get something for Ms. D., so he wrapped his egg in a sheet of notebook paper. "It's a nice gift," he said. "Ms. D. likes eggs, and with an egg around the baby will never feel lonely."

Elliot's present was so big it took up most of the gift table all by itself.

"Ms. D. will expect the best from me," he said smugly, looking with pity at all the smaller gifts.

He glared at Adam Joshua. "Where's your stupid present?" he asked, throwing a little snarl into the smug.

"It's not here yet," Adam Joshua said. He tried to look a little smug himself, but he simply didn't have the talent for it that Elliot did.

Sidney walked in the door and Angie loaded him down with posters and tape. He sighed, then took a shoe off and put his egg in it to keep it safe while he worked.

He taped up a poster that told Ms. D. they'd miss her, another saying they loved her, and he added a personal note on the third telling her she should call off the math test. Sidney stood back to make sure all the posters were nice and straight, then he absentmindedly slipped his foot into his shoe.

There was a terrible crunch followed by a terrible look on Sidney's face.

Everybody watched while yolk oozed up between his toes.

"I absolutely hate this egg project," Sidney said, very sad.

"Somebody's coming!" Heidi told them. Everybody scurried around the room hiding, and the minute they heard someone at the door they jumped out and yelled "Surprise!" just as loudly as they could.

Mrs. Rodriguez stood in the doorway looking scared out of her wits and definitely surprised.

"Thank you very much," she said, trying to catch her breath. "That was a nice way to start the day."

"Oh, my gosh," Sidney shouted. He ran in circles again, making a wet, squishy egg sound. "Ms. D. had the baby! She had the baby!"

Mrs. Rodriguez waited till he'd run himself out.

"Yep!" she told them, laughing. "Last night."

"It's a boy," she said, and the boys all war-whooped it up.

"And a girl," Mrs. Rodriguez shouted over the noise, and the girls all cheered.

Then everybody stopped whooping and cheering and looked totally bewildered.

"Twins?" Angie finally yelped.

"No wonder Ms. D. was so fat," Sidney panted, nodding wisely.

Turning out to be the surprised ones at their own surprise party left everybody feeling a little blue and more than a little confused.

"Does this mean we don't get any cake?" Jonesy asked, eyeing the cake.

"Ms. D. didn't even say good-bye," Angie said, very glum.

"And does this mean we get to keep the presents?" Jonesy asked, eyeing the skateboard.

"This means we're taking our party on the road!" Mrs. Rodriguez told them. "I talked to Philip's father since he's a doctor at the hospital. He arranged things so that we can go, peek at the babies, and use a doctors' lounge for the party."

Everybody cheered and pounded Philip on the back while he stood there looking proud.

"Of course, it didn't hurt that Ms. D. made it very plain she wasn't going to miss this party for the world," Mrs. Rodriguez said, laughing.

"It won't be a surprise so it won't be so exciting," Heidi said, disappointed.

"Trust me," Mrs. Rodriguez said. "I don't think Mr. D. can take any more excitement right now."

Mr. D. came to meet them at the door of the hospital, looking a little glazed around the eyes, trembly in the knees, absolutely exhausted, and totally proud.

"The twins are so little and cute," he said, sounding fatherly. "They look a whole lot like Ms. D. and just a little like me."

"Thank goodness!" said Angie.

"A nurse named Olivia is going to take us down to the nursery window so you can meet the babies," Mrs. Rodriguez said. "But you're to be very calm, very quiet, and try to look like you don't have any germs."

"Nurse Olivia scares me," Mr. D. told them. "She's already scolded me twice."

Nurse Olivia scared everybody.

"March," she told them, leading the way. "On your tiptoes."

Nobody could believe how little the babies were.

"Or how cute," Angie whispered. Everybody tapped lightly on the window and waved at the twins.

Adam Joshua looked the babies over suspiciously. The boy looked like he might turn out to be as great a kid as Ms. D. thought Adam Joshua was. On the other hand, the girl looked like she was going to turn out exactly like Amanda Jane.

"You're never going to be able to tell them apart," said Sidney.

"I got to hold them right away," Mr. D. told them, "right in the delivery room!"

"They let you hold them?" Angie yelped.

"That's just what I said," said the nurse.

"I want to name them Curly and Moe," said Mr. D.

"Not on your life," said the nurse.

Nurse Olivia marched them on their tiptoes down to the doctors' lounge.

"This is going to be a very quiet party," she told them sternly. "Or I'll have to send you packing."

Everybody nodded, wide-eyed and solemn.

"I really mean it," Nurse Olivia said before she went to get Ms. D. "I send noisy doctors packing all the time."

Ms. D. looked very tired but really happy.

"And a whole lot thinner," Sidney told her.

Everyone suddenly felt a little shy. Personally, Adam Joshua had never seen Ms. D. in a bathrobe before.

"The math test is canceled," she said, smiling.

They would have cheered, but Nurse Olivia had a good close eye on them.

Instead they went over and started hugging Ms. D. gently, one by one. Some hugged her because of the babies, and some because of the math test, and some because they'd miss her.

Adam Joshua wanted to say that he was happy about the baby boy and sorry about the girl and most of all that he'd miss Ms. D.

But he finally had to settle for standing in line and giving her a hug he hoped she'd remember for a long time to come.

It was a monumental party.

"I'm a party expert," Mr. D. said, sounding as delighted as he could with his mouth full of cake, "and this one is great!"

Ms. D. kept getting misty around the edges, which nobody had ever seen her do before.

"But my mom said it's because Ms. D.'s so happy," Heidi told everybody. So they all stopped worrying and felt terrific every time

Ms. D. got a little moist.

Mr. D. loved his presents.

"My own bath duck!" he said.

He misted up a little himself over the skateboard.

"I've always wanted one," he said, thrilled. "It will be a big help with the babies around."

Jonesy, Philip, and Sidney all nodded proudly.

Elliot's gift had been too large to bring.

"It's the biggest teddy bear anybody's ever seen," he said importantly.

"Wow!" Mr. D. told him. "That will really impress my stuffed moose, Morose."

"Thank you, Elliot," Ms. D. said. "I know the babies will enjoy a bear."

"Be sure you tell them it's from me, it's the best money can buy, and how much it cost," Elliot said. "I left the price tag on it."

Adam Joshua's present was an envelope.

"Like that was worth waiting for," Elliot snickered.

Ms. D. read the note inside it and looked up, beaming.

"Adam Joshua," she said. "What a wonderful surprise! What a wonderful gift! You know I'd love one of George's puppies! And one of George's puppies will be great with the babies."

Adam Joshua beamed quite a bit himself. Elliot glared.

"Mrs. Sikes said you can be the first to choose a puppy when they're old enough to leave Lucy," Adam Joshua told Ms. D. "Of course they have to be born first. And George said to tell you he'd come himself, but he doesn't think we could get along without him."

"Why don't you choose a puppy when it's time?" Ms. D. said, chuckling. "You know a special dog when you meet one."

"This is terrific," Mr. D. said, very

happy. "He can also be a watch puppy. Morose is tired of trying to be a watch moose all by himself."

Nurse Olivia took Ms. D. back to her room and then came and led everybody else out of the hospital.

"Best party I ever threw," she told them, winking at Adam Joshua as he tip-toed along.

Mr. D. handed out pink and blue bub-ble-gum cigars before everyone left to head back to school.

The nurse took two.

"I always like one after supper," she said.

Chapter Six

When they got back to the school everybody trooped into the office to collect their eggs.

"It was a pleasure to egg-sit," the school secretary told them. "Except I didn't get much work done. The eggs kept wanting to gossip."

Once they were in the classroom everybody had their cigars, and everybody congratulated each other about having twins, and everybody tried to think up names besides Curly and Moe.

"Angie's good," said Angie.

"So's Nate," said Nate.

"I wouldn't name a flea Sidney," said Sidney.

After a while the excitement started wearing off and they started thinking about Ms. D. really being gone. Then they started feeling glum, gloomy, grouchy, abandoned, and totally depressed.

Several glum, gloomy, grouchy people started grumbling.

"But it isn't so bad," Mrs. Rodriguez told them. "We're getting a very nice substitute lined up."

There was a wet scrunch from somewhere in the room.

"So how does she feel about eggs?" asked Philip.

"Ms. D. was a little worried that something unexpected might happen," Mrs. Rodriguez told them. "She left something for each of you so she could say a special good-bye."

Mrs. Rodriguez pulled out one of Ms. D.'s bags.

Sidney screamed.

"It's not another project, is it?" Heidi asked for all of them, and they all looked worried.

"Just notes," Mrs. Rodriguez said, handing them out.

Ms. D. wasn't that good an artist, but she'd drawn a funny little picture of George on the front of Adam Joshua's note.

It was the best picture of George he'd ever seen.

"I'm going to miss you!" Ms. D. had written. "A lot of people count on you as a friend and a leader, so I'm going to count on you to be a terrific leader while I'm gone."

Adam Joshua hadn't realized Ms. D. would be counting on him so much.

It made a difference.

"I'll be checking in with you to make sure everything's great," Ms. D. had written.

Adam Joshua hadn't known about the checking-in part either. That made a big difference too.

There was a P.S.

"Don't let Elliot bully you," it said. "You can handle him much better than you think."

Everybody read their own notes and they all looked smug and proud.

Elliot just looked quiet and more thoughtful, but given that it was Elliot, it was a nice change.

Mrs. Rodriguez sent them out for recess while she went to do some things in the office.

"Adam Joshua," Angie said, catching up

with him as they headed to the playground. "Scarlett and Barney have fallen in love. Isn't that great?"

Adam Joshua thought it sounded absolutely awful, but then he wasn't an egg.

"They want to get married now," Angie told him, delighted. "It's very exciting!"

Adam Joshua had other things on his mind, and this all seemed fairly sudden.

Still, he didn't think it would hurt to let Barney get married if he really wanted to.

Everybody trooped back into the classroom for a wedding.

Angie had a bridal veil ready to go in her backpack.

"Scarlett's not old enough to get married," Sidney told her, sounding suspicious. "She was just a baby yesterday."

"Eggs grow up very fast," Angie said, as she fixed Scarlett's hair and made her into a beautiful bride.

Egg Fu Two was the bridesmaid. Barney chose Nelson's egg, Sneed, to be the best man. He asked Frankenegg to be the flower girl.

"Good grief!" groaned Angie.

Zilch the Third drummed on the desk while everybody sang "Here Comes the Bride."

"The groom better hide," sang Jonesy.

"Okay, now they're married," said Angie.

Adam Joshua had only been to one wedding, but he remembered it as being a lot longer.

Frankenegg tried to kiss the bride and Angie bopped him.

"Well, rats!" Jonesy groaned, checking the damage. "Now I'll have to change his name to Crackenstein."

Jonesy went to borrow some bandages from the school nurse, and when he came back he set to work wrapping up his egg.

"Revenge of the Egg Mummy," he cackled.

"It's been an exciting day, hasn't it, sweetie?" Angie crooned, straightening Scarlett's veil while she kept a nervous eye on Jonesy. "We'll have to make sure we get lots of pictures to show how pretty you look."

"Arghh!" Sidney groaned. He got a glazed, crazed look in his eyes, took off the shoe that had egg all over it, and started limping toward the nursery.

Nate was sitting in Sidney's path. He had his eyes closed and he was humming a jazzy little tune, beating out the rhythm on his desk while his egg, Zilch, rocked and rolled along.

Sidney raised his shoe high and smashed Zilch flat before Nate saw it coming.

Then Sidney turned slowly and looked straight at Scarlett.

Angie let out a scream, grabbed Scarlett, and made a dash for the coatroom.

Sidney limped steadily on, and he picked up quite a few people along the way, dragging them along while they tried to stop him.

By the time Mrs. Rodriguez got back, Angie had locked herself in and Sidney was pounding out a slow, steady beat with his shoe on the coatroom door.

Thoughtful didn't last too long with Elliot. He came over to Adam Joshua's desk as everyone was getting ready to go home.

"With Ms. D. gone, you're all mine," Elliot sneered, giving Adam Joshua a hard push, "and nothing's going to save you."

Adam Joshua turned and walked away. He knew Ms. D. thought he could handle Elliot, but he didn't think it had to be today.

He went to get Barney, but Angie had

beaten him to it.

"He'll be very happy at my house with Scarlett," Angie told Adam Joshua. "Husbands always want to live with their wives," she called back over her shoulder as she bustled the newlyweds out the door.

Adam Joshua and Nelson were fairly quiet and thoughtful themselves on the walk home.

The good thing was that it was time for the weekend, so they wouldn't have to deal with a teacher who wasn't Ms. D. until Monday. The bad thing was that Monday was only three days away.

Adam Joshua sighed. The note had helped, but he was still eggless, Ms. D–less, and nearly dogless, and if anybody wanted to ask he had one too many sisters.

"The cute gets them every time," Nelson said, sighing too.

"Twins," Adam Joshua told George when he got home. "That's just two and Mr. D. looked like he was ready to faint. We're talking five, ten, maybe twenty puppies."

George looked flabbergasted.

He wasn't all that great at counting, but if two was making Mr. D. nearly faint, twenty sounded like something to worry about.

Adam Joshua let George worry. He planned on doing a lot of it himself during the next few days, and it would be nice to have company.

Worrying about things didn't stop them from happening.

On Sunday morning Adam Joshua's mother woke him early.

"Mrs. Sikes just called and asked us to come right over," she said. "They've had a little excitement at their house!"

Adam Joshua pulled the covers up over his head.

There was getting to be more excitement around than he wanted to handle.

Now somebody was probably going to line up a very nice substitute George for him too.

Adam Joshua took his own sweet time getting ready to go to the Sikeses', so everyone else went on ahead.

"Georges," Amanda Jane told Adam Joshua solemnly when he finally made it. She grabbed his hand and pulled him into the kitchen.

George looked like fatherhood had almost been too much for him. But he looked every bit as proud as Mr. D., and every bit as happy, and also fairly relieved that it hadn't been twenty.

There were five brand-new puppies curled up in a basket. Two of them looked just like Lucy.

Two of them looked just like George.

The smallest looked partly like George and partly like Lucy, but not necessarily all the best parts.

Adam Joshua had never known anything so little could be so ugly and cute at the same time.

"Zedda," Amanda Jane said softly, cuddling up beside Adam Joshua. George cuddled up on his other side.

The puppies' eyes were still scrunched shut, but the smallest one raised its head a little shakily and yawned.

Adam Joshua fought against the feeling as long as he could, but there were some things you couldn't win.

He ran his finger down the soft back of the littlest puppy while he sang his father's song.

And to his own great surprise he fell firmly and absolutely in love.